Illustrations by Cameron Wilson for Soulsimplicity Design and Publishing.
for illustration inquires visit camdaillastrata.com.

ENTERING

MY BOOK OF

VIBRANCE

BY JESSE JORDAN

ILLUSTRATED BY CAMERON WILSON

Being different makes us stand out.

One sunny afternoon, my mom took me shopping for new clothes. I discovered that I like to style myself according to the colors and how I feel.

I wear pink when I go to the park with my friends. It makes me feel playful and kind. Always be kind.

I wear blue on the days that I walk my dog. It makes me feel cool and confident. Always be confident.

I wear orange when I
want to step out of my
comfort zone. Always
be brave.

I wear purple when I'm feeling creative and want to explore art. Use your imagination.

I wear red when I
am focused and trying
to reach my goals. Be
determined and eager
to learn.

I wear green when I want to be by myself. It's okay to be alone.

I wear yellow when I
am feeling cheerful.
Be happy.

I wear all the vibrant colors when I am feeling like myself. Be yourself.

PAPER DOLL ACTIVITY

COLOR AND DRESS UP!

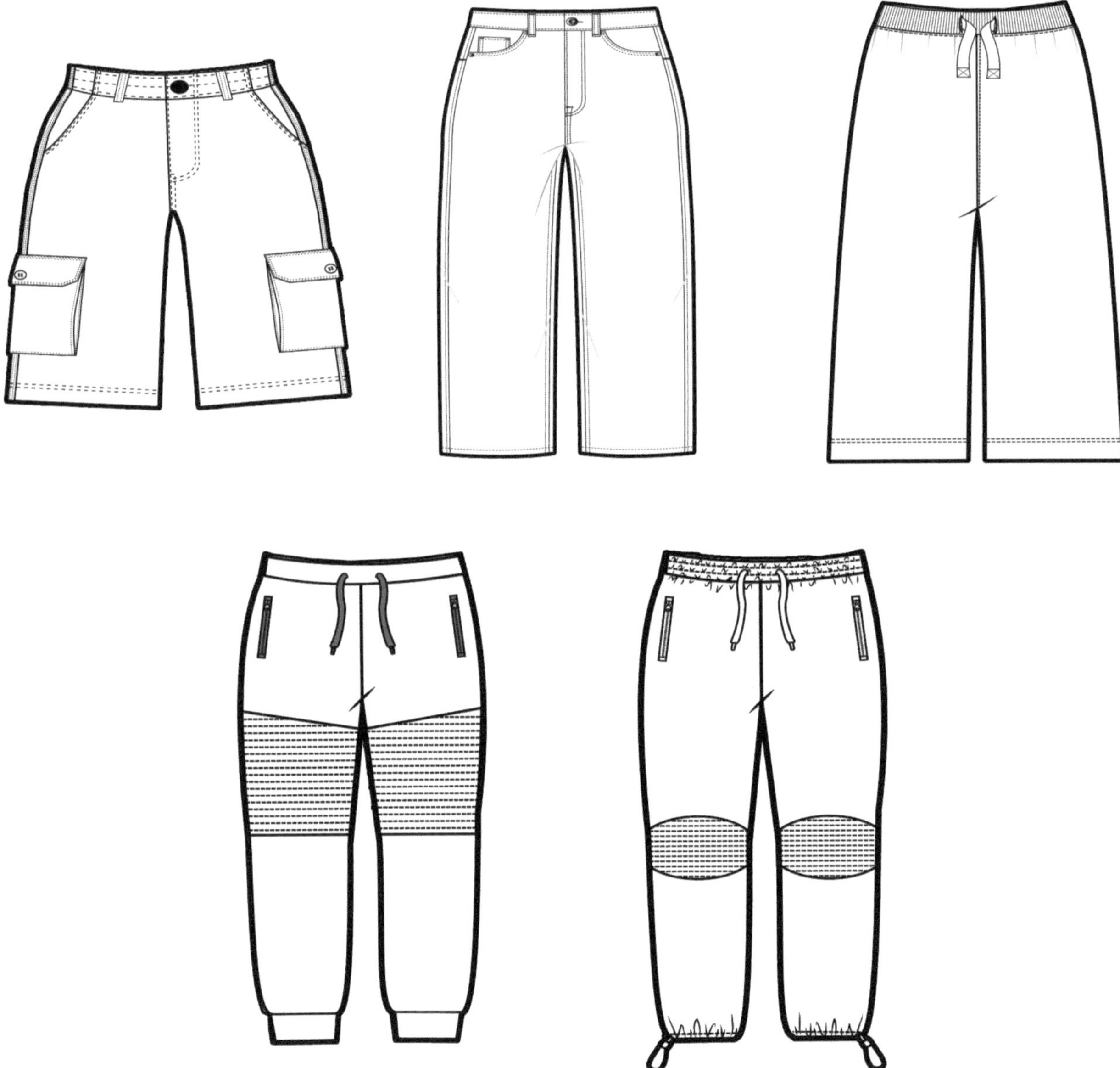